Adapted by **BROOKE VITALE**

Based on the series created by **HARLAND WILLIAMS**

Illustrated by the **DISNEY STORYBOOK ART TEAM**

Los Angeles • New York

First Paperback Edition, May 2019 10 9 8 7 6 5 4 3 2
ISBN 978-1-368-02787-8
FAC-025393-19158
Library of Congress Control Number: 2018955987

Printed in China
For more Disney Press fun, visit www.disneybooks.com

Bob is looking for something.
"I lost my lucky nickel," he says.

Bob looks under a hat.
He looks under the mat.

He even
looks under a **plate**.

"Did you hear that?" Bingo asks.
"Bob lost his lucky pickle!" Rolly
says. "Let's go!"

The pups go to collar up.
Bingo will bring his lucky bone.

Rolly will
bring his lucky **sock**.

The pups are ready
for their mission.

First the pups go to the park.
Rolly finds a stick.

Bingo finds some **noodles**.

The pups see something
behind a tree.

But it is not Bob's lucky pickle.

It is a **balloon**.

The pups keep looking.
They see something running by.
They want to chase it.

It is a **cat**
wearing a **shirt**!

Bingo and Rolly end up at the beach.
Rolly tries to find the lucky pickle.

Bingo sees
something
float by.

It is a **boat**.

Bingo and Rolly head home.
They search the yard.

Rolly sees
something by the  **hose**.

But it is not a
lucky pickle.
It is just an old coin.

Bob comes outside.
"You found my lucky nickel!"
he says.
Bob said "nickel," not "pickle"!

MISSION
ACCOMPLISHED